The Story of Nian
a Folk Tale from China

Written by Dr Wee Bee Geok

Illustrated by Turine Tran

Collins

Chapter 1

Long ago in China, there was a terrible creature called Nian, which lived deep in the ocean. It had a huge body covered in spiky scales, and sharp horns on its long head. Its powerful pointed tail could shatter a boat with just one swoosh.

Nian didn't often come up from the water. But when it did,
sailors shone their lights and blasted their horns to warn
other ships and nearby villages about the creature.
Only then did it quickly sink back into the sea.
The fish nearby had to hide in the corals and reeds
so that the monster didn't eat them in one gulp.

Thankfully, for most of the time, Nian stayed at the bottom
of the ocean.

Chapter 2

However, on the eve of every Chinese New Year,
Nian clambered onto the shore and terrorised the villages.
It attacked the village folk. It charged at the animals.
It gobbled up the crops and destroyed whatever was in
its path. Then it looked for other villages to attack.

Everyone cried, "Run! Run!" as they heard its stomping
footsteps approach.

People fled from the villages to the mountains to escape from the beast. When they returned after the monster had gone, they saw everything in ruins.

Many of the houses were flattened. The grains in the barns were scattered all around and the crops in the farms were destroyed. The animals that the villagers had left behind were found killed or injured. It was a sad, sorry sight.

Chapter 3

One Chinese New Year's Eve, like every other before that, the villagers of Little Rock were preparing to flee to the mountains to hide from Nian.

They shut up their houses, putting bars across the entrances. They locked away their harvested crops in the barns and took enough food with them to survive the night. They herded their sheep, goats, chickens and ducks onto carts. Then the villagers gathered the children and hurried away from the village, their carts creaking as they moved along the pebbly path.

Dusk fell, and the wind whipped around them. The animals grunted and bleated in protest at having to leave their homes.

"Mama, I don't like this!" wailed a young girl, clutching her teddy bear.

Her mother whispered, "It's all right, sweetie. Don't be afraid. We have to go away for now, but we'll be back tomorrow."

"What's going on, Papa?" asked a scared little boy, as he ran along beside a cart.

"Son, be brave," his father said. "We're going to the mountains, just for tonight, to keep out of the way of Nian, the monster from the sea."

Chapter 4

As they continued along the bumpy path, a grey-haired
man in a red cloak appeared from amongst the bushes.
The stranger had a long flowing beard and a twinkle in
his eyes. He looked calmly at the scene before him and said,
"Let me stay here one night and I'll get rid
of Nian for you."

"Are you mad, old man?" the little boy's father shouted. "For years, no one has been able to stop the monster. What makes you think you can? You must come to the mountains with us."

"No, I'm not going with you," the old man replied.

"Do you know how cruel Nian is? It'll tear you to pieces. Just jump onto this cart here and we'll take you with us." The little boy's father tried to change the old man's mind, but it was no use. He shook his head and started walking towards the ocean.

The villagers had no choice but to leave for the mountains
without him. The little girl kept looking back hopefully,
but the old man didn't follow. Instead, he stared at
the indigo sea, waiting … and waiting for Nian to appear.
But he knew the creature would only
emerge when that day ended
and the new one began.

Chapter 5

The old man hurried away to set his plan into action,
returning moments before the stroke of midnight.
He watched the sea rumble, sending waves crashing
onto the shore. With a deafening roar, Nian's horned
head rose out from the sea.

The man clenched his teeth at the sight of the scaly creature as it slowly clambered from the water and made its way to the village. *Clomp! Clomp! Clomp!* It swung its head around, preparing to attack.

But as it drew closer to the village, it heard loud bursts of explosion, which rattled like thunder in its ears. *Boom! Bang! Bang!*

Fiery sparks came from nowhere, blinding the monster. The creature clamped its eyes shut, and kept stomping.

Nian didn't know the sparks came from the old man in the red cloak. He'd guessed Nian was scared of bright lights and loud noises, because it always fled from the sailors' spotlights and horns at sea. He stood in front of the rows of mud-walled houses of the village, firing a stream of firecrackers at the creature. *Boom! Bang! Bang!*

"Be gone, monster! Leave us alone!" he shouted. He told himself not to be scared, although he could feel beads of cold sweat covering his forehead.

He saw Nian tremble as the fiery sparks rained down, and the creature ran towards the houses to hide, yelling, "Aagghh!"

Chapter 6

As soon as Nian reached the houses, it sank to the ground, shivering with fear. The wooden doors of the houses were not their normal dull brown. Instead, they were red from top to bottom.

Like the firecrackers, this was the work of the old man.
His own house, in a nearby village, was a meeting place,
and it had red flags outside. Although the monster
had also attacked that village, it'd always left
the old man's house alone. The old man guessed that
Nian hated red, and so he'd stuck strips of red paper
across every single door in this village.

Yelping in fright, the creature ran away from the red doors
as fast as its scaly legs could carry it.

The old man watched, clapping his hands in delight. But there was no time to stop – he heard another howl from the monster. It came from the barns – loud, long and screeching.

The old man had filled the barns with bright lanterns.
He found Nian shuddering in front of the bright lights,
its eyes shut tight. Unlike the monster, the old man
wasn't afraid. He took a deep breath and stepped
towards it, even though it was many times
his size.

"Leave us alone! Stop frightening our villagers!" he yelled. "I'm not scared of you. And if you ever attack a village again, I'll do things to give you nightmares forever!"

Nian opened its shrivelled eyes for a moment, and the old man stared deep into its pupils. They were tiny now, full of fear. The creature breathed hard, raised itself up slowly, and stumbled away from the barns towards the sea.

Chapter 7

As Nian's howls of "Ahooo! Ahooo!" faded into the distance, the old man jumped for joy. He sat down for a moment on a sack of grain and looked around at the untouched barn. His old, wrinkled hands trembled with happiness.
He'd defeated the Nian monster!

"This evil creature has learnt its lesson," he told himself.
"It'll never trouble the villagers again."

The old man took one last look at the bright, burning
lanterns and the red-covered doors, and beamed.
He walked down the path and out of
the village, whistling.

Chapter 8

When the villagers began making their way back down the mountain the next day, they saw the bright lights and spots of red in the distance and wondered what had happened.

They started running down the hill, looking for signs of the monster. But when they rounded the corner and saw their houses up close, they cried out in amazement.

Nothing was destroyed! Their houses were undamaged –
not one window was smashed, not one door broken.
Instead, they were all covered in red! The sacks in the barns
were still full of grain, lit up by bright lanterns. The crops in
the fields were untouched, swaying in the breeze.
The animals that they'd left behind were unharmed –
the cows mooing in the fields, the calves
munching grass.

The villagers couldn't believe their eyes. The old man was true to his words. He'd stopped Nian destroying their village.

They looked for the man in the red cloak to thank him. They wanted to ask how he knew what Nian was scared of, but he was gone. However, they didn't forget him. Tales of how the old man defeated the monster spread from village to village, far and wide. Finally, people were no longer afraid of Nian.

Chapter 9

From that day onwards, on the eve of Chinese New Year, Chinese families celebrate the passing of Nian by hanging red banners on their doors and keeping their homes brightly lit throughout the night. Everyone – men, women and children – stay up late to watch firecrackers being set off at midnight.

And what became of the Nian monster? It never dared raise itself out of the ocean again.

Monster against man

Ideas for reading

Written by Clare Dowdall, PhD
Lecturer and Primary Literacy Consultant

Reading objectives:
- identify themes and conventions
- discuss words and phrases that capture the reader's interest and imagination
- draw inferences and justify these with evidence
- make predictions from details stated and applied

Spoken language objectives:
- use spoken language to develop understanding through speculating, hypothesising, imagining and exploring ideas

Curriculum links: Geography – locational knowledge

Resources: ICT; example willow plate; map of the world

Build a context for reading
- Help children locate China on a map and share any knowledge they have about the country.
- Ask children what they know about how New Year is celebrated in China, and whether they have seen Chinese New Year celebrations.
- Look at the front cover and read the title. Discuss what can be seen and discuss whether folk tales are fact or fiction.
- Read the blurb to the children. Ask them to predict how the villagers might stop the Nian monster from attacking their village.

Understand and apply reading strategies
- Read pp2–3 to the children. Ask them to close their eyes and visualise Nian as you read.
- Challenge children to describe him in their own words, making inferences, and to use the five senses to extend their descriptions.